Billy on the Building Site

John Talbot

A & C BLACK · LONDON

For Louis

First published 1986 by A & C Black (Publishers) Ltd
35 Bedford Row, London WC1R 4JH
Copyright © 1986 John Talbot
Printed in Singapore by Tien Wah Press (Pte) Ltd

British Library Cataloguing in Publication Data
Talbot, John
Billy on the building site.
I. Title
823.914   [J]   PZ7

ISBN 0-7136-2658-5

"Good Morning!"

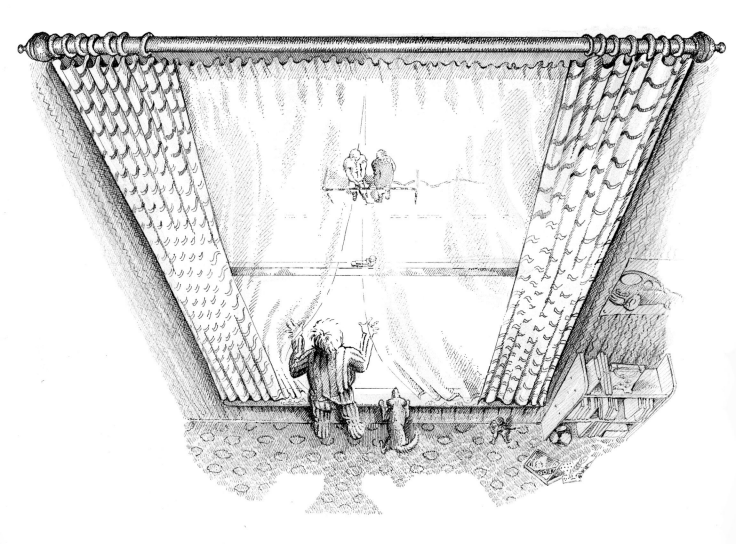

"Look, there are our friends Mick and Pat."

"Hello there Billy." "Hello."

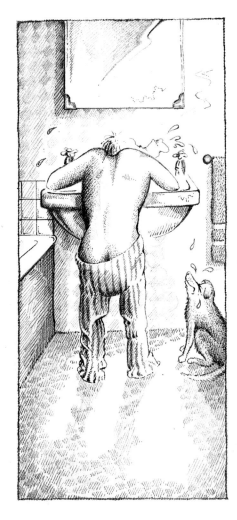  

"Hurry up Tag."

"Let's go out and see them."

"Would you do us a favour Billy?"

"That was kind of him to go for the milk."

"Slow down Tag!"

"Where have they gone?"

"No, they're not in there."

"No ... No ... No ... No ."

"Where are they?"

"Oh look, can you see them?"

"Stay there, we'll be down for a cup!"

"I think he said, 'Come on up'."

"Hey! Wait for me."

"Phew, almost there."

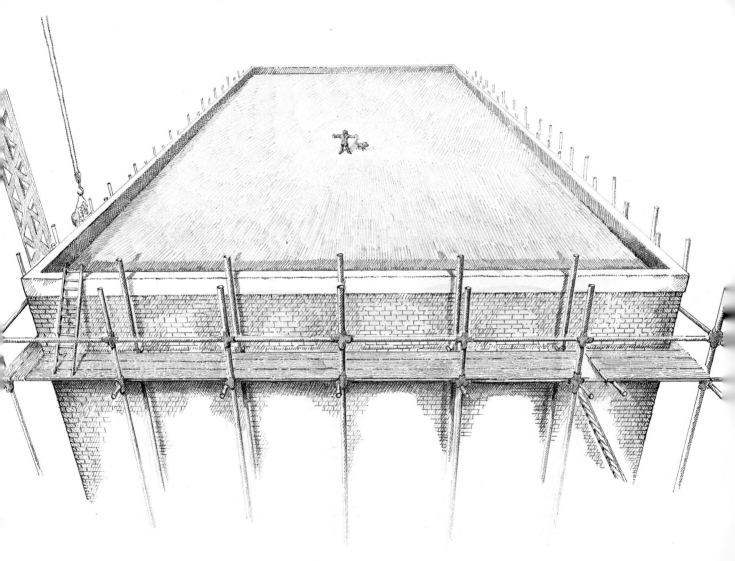

"Where have they gone?"

"Oh well, down again."

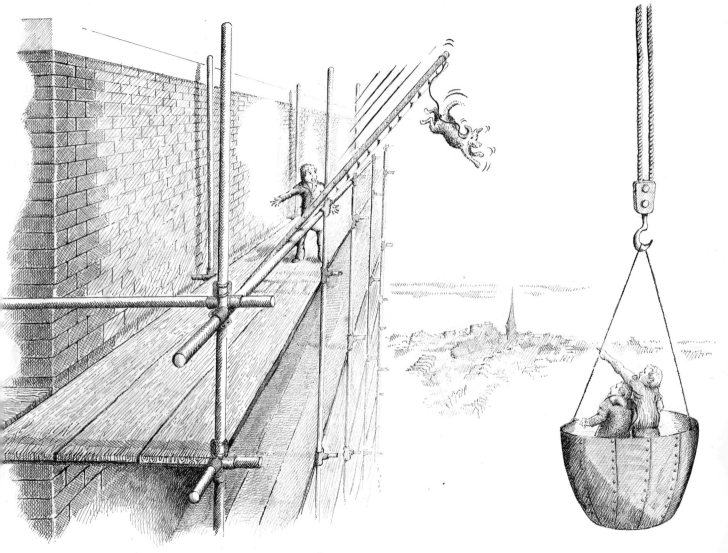

"Look out Tag!"

"Quick! Swing us over!"

.... Nurrrrrrrrrrrr....

"GO BACK BILLY! GO BACK! We'll get him!"

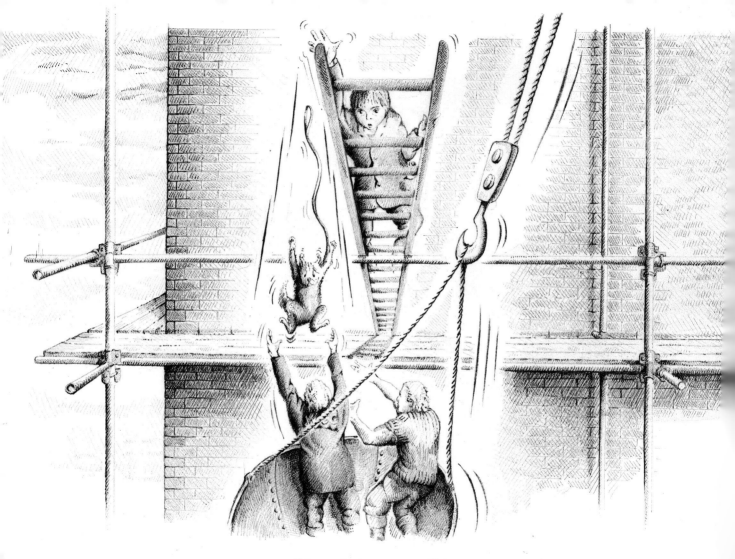

"Catch him Pat!"

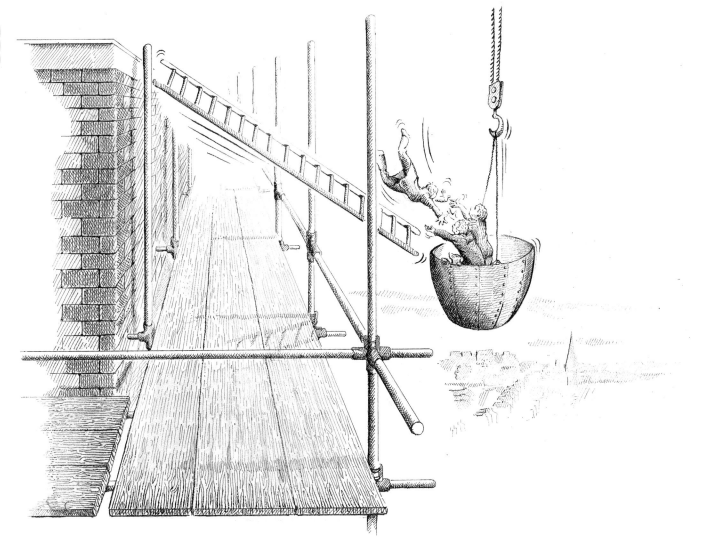

"Ahhhhhhhhhhhhhhhh!"

"Hang on Billy – we've got you!"

"Sure he's a grand lad! . . . and he didn't even spill the milk."

"Look Tag!"

"There's our house."

"Perhaps Billy would get the milk for us every morning . . . hey Pat?"